The Lost Voice

Written by Cynthia Rider
based on the original characters
created by Roderick Hunt and Alex Brychta
Illustrated by Alex Brychta

OXFOR
UNIVERSITY P

Chip didn't feel very well. His throat
was sore and he couldn't talk.

"Chip has lost his voice," said Dad.

"Oh no!" thought Floppy.

Mum took Chip to the doctor.

Dad took Biff and Kipper to school.

Floppy was all on his own.

"Chip has lost his voice," he
thought sadly. "I wish I could help
him."

"I know!" thought Floppy.
"I'll go and find Chip's
voice. I'm good at
finding things."

8

He wagged his tail
and ran upstairs.

Floppy ran into Chip's bedroom.
He looked under the bed. He found
a ball, a toy car, a sticky sweet and
a dusty sock . . .

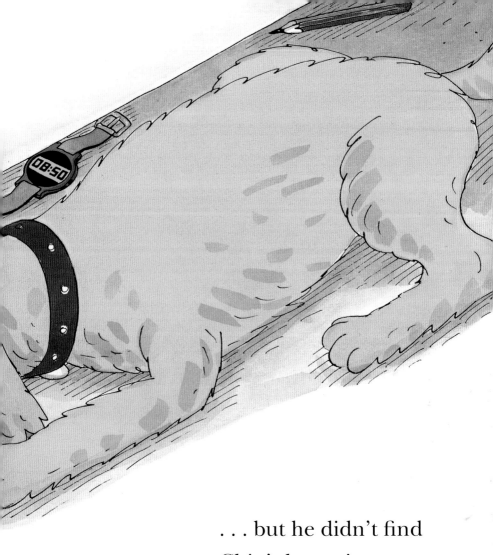

. . . but he didn't find
Chip's lost voice.

Floppy looked in the toy box.
He found lots of toys and lots
of books . . .

. . . but he didn't find
Chip's lost voice.

Suddenly, the phone rang.
"There are voices in the phone,"
thought Floppy. "I bet Chip's voice
is in there."

Floppy hit the phone with his paw.
CRASH! It fell down. A voice said,
"Hello! Is anyone there?"
But it wasn't Chip's voice.

Floppy looked at the radio. "There
are voices in the radio," he thought.
"I bet Chip's voice is in there."

He hit the radio with his paw.

Nothing happened. He hit it harder

. . . and harder!

CRASH! The radio fell over
and someone started to sing.

"What a horrible noise," thought
Floppy. "That isn't Chip."

"I bet Chip's voice is in the television," thought Floppy. He ran to look. His paw hit the switch and the television came on.

Floppy saw a dog on the television.
It ran out of a shop with a big bone.

"Wow! That bone looks good,"
thought Floppy.

The dog ran faster and faster. A
voice shouted, "Stop! Stop that dog!"

"That isn't Chip," thought Floppy,
and he went back upstairs.

Floppy saw Teddy on Kipper's bed.
"Teddy!" he thought. "I bet Teddy
has got Chip's voice."

Floppy shook Teddy hard.

Grrrrrrrr! growled Teddy.

"Help!" barked Floppy. He dropped
Teddy and ran into Biff's bedroom.

WHOOSH! Floppy went skidding across the floor.

CRASH! Biff's clock fell over. "Wake up!" it shouted.

Floppy was scared. He hid under
Chip's bed and shut his eyes. Soon,
he was fast asleep.

Chip came home. He was feeling
a lot better now.

"Where are you, Floppy?" he called.

Floppy jumped up. "Chip has found his voice!" he thought.

He wagged his tail and ran downstairs.

Just then, Biff came in. Her throat
was sore and she couldn't talk.

"Biff has lost her voice," said Dad.

"Oh no!" thought Floppy.

Talk about the story

Why did Dad say that Chip had lost his voice?

Where did Floppy look for Chip's voice?

What do you think happened next?

What would Floppy find if he looked under your bed?

Hidden words

Help Floppy to get his bone by finding the words hidden within the words on the stairs, like this: h**is**